HEIDI HECKELBECK

Casts a Spell

By Wanda Coven
Illustrated by Priscilla Burris

LITTLE SIMON
New York London Toronto Sydney New Delhi

LITTLE SIMON
An imprint of Simon & Schuster Children's Publishing Division
1230 Avenue of the Americas, New York, New York 10020
Copyright © 2012 by Simon & Schuster, Inc.
All rights reserved, including the right of reproduction in whole or in part in any form.
LITTLE SIMON is a registered trademark of Simon & Schuster, Inc., and associated colophon is a trademark of Simon & Schuster, Inc.
For information about special discounts for bulk purchases, please contact Simon & Schuster Special Sales at 1-866-506-1949 or business@simonandschuster.com.
The Simon & Schuster Speakers Bureau can bring authors to your live event. For more information or to book an event contact the Simon & Schuster Speakers Bureau at 1-866-248-3049 or visit our website at www.simonspeakers.com.
Manufactured in the United States of America 0616 MTN
20 19 18 17 16 15 14 13
Library of Congress Cataloging-in-Publication Data
Coven, Wanda.
Heidi Heckelbeck casts a spell / by Wanda Coven ; illustrated by Priscilla Burris.
— 1st ed.
p. cm.
Summary: Second-grade witch Heidi Heckelbeck wants revenge against Melanie, the meanest girl in school, so she decides to cast a forgetting spell on her right before the start of the school play.
ISBN 978-1-4424-3567-4 (pbk.)
ISBN 978-1-4424-4088-3 (hardcover)
[etc.]
[1. Witches—Fiction. 2. Conduct of life—Fiction. 3. Schools—Fiction.]
I. Burris, Priscilla, ill. II. Title.
PZ7.C83392Hc 2012
[Fic]—dc23
2011014336
ISBN 978-1-4424-3568-1 (eBook)

CONTENTS

A SPELL FOR SMELL-A-NiE

Abracadabra!

Alakazam!

Presto change-o!

Heidi Heckelbeck flipped open her *Book of Spells*. The book had been a gift from her grandmother, who was a witch. Heidi's mother was also a witch, as well as her Aunt Trudy and, of course, Heidi. Heidi's dad and little brother, Henry, were just regular people.

The book's worn pages crinkled as she thumbed through them.

"Bingo!" Heidi said to herself.

She had found the spell:

How to Make Someone Forget

Heidi had discovered it last night. Tucked inside the page was a piece of paper. Heidi unfolded it. It was a list of all the rotten things Melanie Maplethorpe had done to Heidi on her first day of school yesterday.

Mean Things Melanie Did to Me

1. She called me smelly.

2. She gave me five dirty looks for no reason!

3. She put a jack-o'-lantern face on my self-portrait.

4. She made me get cast as a scary apple tree in the class play.

"I'm going to teach Princess Smell-a-nie a lesson once and for all," said Heidi.

In three weeks Heidi's second-grade class would be performing *The Wizard of Oz*. Heidi planned to cast the spell on opening night.

Imagine how meanie Melanie will feel when she forgets all her lines, thought Heidi. She could hardly wait.

Heidi studied the list of ingredients she would need for the spell.

1 eye of a gingerbread man

1 black plastic spider

1 piece of straw

1 teaspoon of salt

3 cornflakes

2 sour gummy worms

1 puppy tooth

1 tablespoon of catnip

3 splashes of water

Wow, thought Heidi. *Where am I going to find all this stuff?* It would be a treasure hunt, that was for sure. She copied the ingredients onto a piece of paper and stuck it in her pocket. Then she read the directions carefully.

Mix ingredients together in a red sand pail. Close your eyes and place one hand over the pail.

Hold your Witches of Westwick medallion in your other hand. Chant the following words:

Oh, Special juice,
Let your Powers loose!
Help Me quickly,
show Me soon The signs.
Make [name of Person]
Forget [his or her] lines!

I'd better get started, thought Heidi.

Chapter 2

CRUNCHY, SALTY WAFFLES

Heidi stashed the *Book of Spells* in her keepsake box and shoved it under the bed. Then she found a silver drawstring pouch that would hold her spell ingredients. The pouch had been a gift from Aunt Trudy. She tied it to her belt loop and dashed downstairs to the kitchen, where mom and Henry were waiting.

Mom had made waffles for breakfast. She placed a waffle and orange slices in front of Heidi.

"You know what I'm in the mood for?" asked Heidi.

"Let me guess," said Mom. "Not waffles."

"Cornflakes," said Heidi.

Heidi's mother raised an eyebrow.

"Haven't you heard?" asked Mom. "You hate cornflakes."

"I know," said Heidi, "but I'm craving crunchy waffles."

"Me too!" said Henry.

Heidi rolled her eyes.

"Do you even know what 'crave' means?" asked Heidi.

"Yup," said Henry. "It means you absolutely have to have something or else you'll go bananas."

"Wow, you're smarter than I thought," said Heidi.

Mom set a box of cornflakes on the table.

Heidi sprinkled some on her waffles.

Then she snuck a few into her pouch.

Now she needed salt. But first she had to distract Henry.

"Cool-o!" said Heidi. "There's a maze on the back of the cereal box!"

"Let me see!" said Henry.

Heidi slid the cereal box to Henry.

He studied the maze while he ate.

Heidi grabbed the saltshaker. She unscrewed the top and poured some into her pouch. Then she put the saltshaker back on the table.

Henry looked up. "Hey, Mom," he said. "Heidi just put salt on her crunchy waffles!"

"So?" said Heidi.

"So that's gross," said Henry.

Then Dad walked into the kitchen.
"I like salt on my waffles too," said
Dad. "And ketchup and bacon."

Heidi and Henry groaned.
"Okay, okay," said Mom. "Hop to it,
kiddos, or you'll miss the bus!"

Chapter 3

BRUCE

Heidi looked for some of the spell ingredients on the way to the bus stop. She didn't see a piece of straw or a single puppy tooth along the way. *How am I supposed to find a puppy tooth, anyway?* she wondered. Heidi had never seen one lying around before. Did puppies even lose their teeth? Heidi had no idea, but she absolutely had to have one to complete her spell.

"Woo-hoo!" a voice called. "Heidi! Henry!"

Aunt Trudy waved from her porch. Her cottage looked like a gingerbread house with pink and green trim. She had on a bathrobe and held a cup of tea in her hand. Her red hair was the same color as Heidi's, only Aunt Trudy wore hers in a braid. Heidi loved Aunt Trudy. She learned all kinds of cool witchy stuff from her—stuff that her mother would not share.

"Come visit me after school!" Aunt Trudy sang.

"Sure thing!" said Heidi, waving back.

Henry waved too.

The school bus pulled to the curb a few houses up. Heidi and Henry ran like crazy to catch it.

Henry hopped on board and sat next to his new friend Dudley. Henry had only taken the bus once, but he acted like an old pro. This was Heidi's first time, since her mom had given her a ride yesterday. Heidi looked around for her friend Lucy Lancaster. Lucy had been nice to Heidi on her first day of school, but there was no sign of Lucy on the bus. Then she noticed Lucy's friend Bruce Bickerson. Bruce had short brown hair and wore tortoiseshell glasses. The seat beside him was empty. Heidi tried to act cool

as she walked up the aisle. Then she sat down next to Bruce.

"Hey," said Bruce.

"Hey," said Heidi.

The bus groaned as it began to move.

"So why'd you leave your old school, anyway?" asked Bruce.

"I didn't have an old school," said Heidi. "My mom homeschooled my brother and me."

"That's so cool!" said Bruce. "Did you watch TV and play games whenever you felt like it?"

"No way," said Heidi. "We had a strict schedule, but sometimes we got to have school in our pajamas."

"Sounds comfy," said Bruce. "So, are you excited about the school play?"

"Not really," said Heidi.

"Me neither," said Bruce. "I'd rather

be working on my sticker tracker."

"What's a sticker tracker?" asked Heidi.

"It's a special sticker I invented," said Bruce. "You can stick it on letters, people—even pets. Then you can track the object on a webcam. I call it the Bicker Sticker."

"That's neat," said Heidi. "Have you tested it?"

"Yeah, I tested it on my puppy," said Bruce. "I saw him dig up my mom's tulip bulbs from my laboratory."

"You have a puppy?" asked Heidi. "And a laboratory?"

"Yup," said Bruce. "He's a white lab named Benjamin Franklin, but we call him Frankie for short. My laboratory is in the basement."

"Has Frankie lost any teeth?" asked Heidi eagerly.

"Not yet," said Bruce.

"Can I have one if he does?" asked Heidi.

"I guess so," said Bruce.

"I'll trade you a shark tooth for a puppy tooth," said Heidi.

"Deal!" said Bruce.

"Will you promise to check his puppy bed every day?" asked Heidi.

"Promise," said Bruce. "I'll track him with a Bicker Sticker too!"

They shook on it.

Heidi felt pretty good for a change, but the feeling only lasted for about a

second because soon she heard a . . .

WHACK!

A backpack smacked Bruce in the back of the head.

"Owee!" yelped Bruce.

His eyeglasses sailed across two seats and landed in the aisle.

Heidi gasped.

Who would do such a rotten thing? she wondered.

It must've been meanie Melanie. She whipped around to get a good look.

Chapter 4

TOADS AND MICE

When Heidi turned around, she came face-to-face with a squinty-eyed boy with a pug nose and freckles. He gave Heidi the evil eye. Heidi turned right back around. Her friend Bruce had his arms out like a zombie and was grasping the air. Poor Bruce! He couldn't see a thing without his glasses.

"Bickerson's *blind*!" said the bully as he laughed.

Heidi spotted Bruce's glasses on the floor. She dove down and grabbed them. As she crawled back to her seat Heidi noticed the bully's sneakers. She

gently tugged the laces and untied them. Then she jumped to her feet and handed the glasses to Bruce.

"Thanks," he said.

"No problem," said Heidi.

Kids began to file off the bus. The bully shoved his way down the aisle. But before he could get to the stairs, he tripped over his shoelaces and stumbled to the ground.

Everyone clapped and laughed.

"Did you have something to do with that?" asked Bruce.

"Maybe," said Heidi.

Bruce held up his right hand and Heidi slapped him five.

"Who was that, anyway?" asked

Heidi as they made their way off the bus.

"Travis Templeton," said Bruce. "He's a fifth grader and the biggest bully in the whole school."

Wow, thought Heidi. *School was much easier at home.*

The morning seemed to whiz by. Melanie held her nose whenever she saw Heidi, but nothing else bad happened.

Heidi had lunch with Bruce and Lucy. Next she yawned her way through drama class. When school was finally over, she was able to visit Aunt Trudy.

Heidi ran from the bus stop to Aunt Trudy's and rang the bell. Aunt Trudy's parrots squawked in the kitchen. She opened the door and gave

Heidi a squeeze. Heidi got a whiff of flowers, tea, and spice. Aunt Trudy ran a mail-order perfume business from home. She made all her perfumes and witch's brews in her kitchen.

"Come on in!" sang Aunt Trudy. "I made apple cider."

Heidi brushed through the beaded
curtains that led into the living room.

She took off her coat and sat down on the couch. Aunt Trudy's cats, Agnes and Hilda, jumped onto her lap.

Aunt Trudy sat down on a soft, mushroom-shaped stool. She gave Heidi some gingersnaps and apple cider.

"So, how's school going?" asked Aunt Trudy.

"Not so great," said Heidi.

"I know it's hard being new," said Aunt Trudy. "Tell me about it."

Heidi told Aunt Trudy about meanie Melanie and how she had gotten Heidi cast as a scary tree in the class play.

She also told her about the bully on the school bus.

"Give Melanie time," said Aunt Trudy. "She's not used to having a new girl in class. As for the bully, just ignore him. I bet if you do, he'll stop bothering you."

"I wish I could cast a spell on both of them," said Heidi. "By the way, do you have a black plastic spider?"

Aunt Trudy laughed at first. She knew exactly what Heidi was up to. But then she sighed and looked at Heidi with a raised eyebrow.

"You must be careful with your powers," said Aunt Trudy. "You can't turn people into toads and mice—or make them forget—just because they make you mad."

"I just want to scare Melanie," said Heidi. "I would reverse the spell after the play."

"Witches have to solve their problems without magic first," said Aunt Trudy. "That's why they go to school."

"Have you ever practiced magic on your customers?" asked Heidi.

"Never," said Aunt Trudy. "And you must promise me you'll never use magic at school."

Maybe her aunt was right. Maybe Heidi should just learn how to get along with others.

"Okay," agreed Heidi, but she was careful not to promise.

After their snack, Aunt Trudy had

to get back to work. She gave Heidi a hug and asked her to take out the trash before she left. Heidi carried the paper bag of trash to the barrel. On the way she noticed a cat toy on the top of the trash. She pulled it out and felt it with her fingers. It felt like it was stuffed with pine needles. Then she sniffed it.

Catnip! thought Heidi. *That's one*

of the spell ingredients. She decided to take the cat toy with her, just in case. She stuffed it in her pouch and dumped the paper bag into the barrel.

Then she ran down the sidewalk for home.

Chapter 5

TIM-BER!

Heidi stopped thinking about casting spells and worked on getting along with others. When Melanie made fun of her clothes, Heidi ignored her. When Travis gave her the evil eye, she pretended not to notice. And when Lucy wanted to be first on the monkey bars, Heidi let her go first. Heidi was

a good citizen for three whole weeks!
But then everything went bonkers at
dress rehearsal.

Heidi rubbed brown face paint on
her face and hands to look like tree

bark. Then she helped Lucy stuff her
curly dark hair into an old-lady wig.

"Hello, Auntie Em!" said Heidi.

Lucy laughed.

"You should see my Munchkin wig," said Lucy.

She pulled another wig from her backpack. It had orange curlicue hair with a rubber bald patch in front.

"Scary, right?" said Lucy.

Heidi laughed so hard she snorted.

"What's so funny?" asked Bruce.
Heidi and Lucy turned around.

Bruce had on silver face paint, silver
clothes, and a kitchen funnel on top
of his head. He held a plastic ax in his

hand. The girls laughed even harder.

"I'm the Tin Man," said Bruce. "So what?"

"So you look like you belong in a junkyard!" said Lucy.

"Well, *you* look like you belong in an old folk's home!" said Bruce.

"And Heidi looks like she belongs in a pigsty," said Melanie.

Melanie was wearing her Dorothy costume, but she acted like the Wicked Witch.

Mrs. Noddywonks, their drama teacher, clapped her hands.

"Please put on your costume, Heidi," she said.

Heidi joined two other students who were scary apple trees. They

already had on their costumes. Mrs. Noddywonks lowered the cardboard tree trunk over Heidi's body. Heidi could barely move. She had to twist the trunk to find the hole for her face. Then she poked her arms through the holes in either side of the tree.

"Hold your arms in the air like branches," said Mrs. Noddywonks.

Heidi held up her arms. She felt like a total ding-dong.

"Places please, everyone!" called

Mrs. Noddywonks. "Now let's start by practicing the apple tree scene."

"Come on, Stanley!" said Melanie.

Her ruby slippers clacked down the stairs in front of the stage. She held a basket with a stuffed Toto peeking out.

Stanley Stonewrecker had the part
of the Scarecrow. He was Melanie's
closest friend.

"Action!" said Mrs. Noddywonks.

Dorothy ran up the stairs onto the
stage.

"Oh, look!" she said. "Apples!"

She tried to pick an apple from one

of the trees, but it slapped her hand.

"Ouch!" cried Dorothy.

"Get your grubby paws off my apples!" said the tree.

"Did you say something?" asked Dorothy. "We don't have talking trees in Kansas!"

"Go pick on someone else!" said the tree.

"Yeah!" said the second tree.

Heidi watched from the hole in her tree.

"Come on, Dorothy," said the Scarecrow. "You don't want to eat *those* wormy apples."

"How dare you make fun of my apples!" said the first tree. "Fire away, guys!"

The trees launched their Styrofoam apples.

Dorothy and the Scarecrow dodged the apples. They also picked up a few for Dorothy's basket. When Dorothy stood up, she bumped one of Heidi's

branches on purpose. Heidi's costume
shifted to one side.

"Help!" cried Heidi. "I can't see!"

She teetered one way and then
tottered the other. She turned in

circles, and then *splat!* Heidi tipped over on center stage.

"*Tim-ber!*" said Melanie. She nudged Stanley and they both laughed.

Heidi could hear Mrs. Noddywonks

scurry across the stage. She pulled
Heidi's costume off.

"Are you okay, dear?" asked
Mrs. Noddywonks.

Heidi's hair was tangled and
stuck to her face paint. She felt too
embarrassed to notice if she was hurt.

"I'm fine," said Heidi.

But Heidi wasn't fine, she was FURIOUS.

That Melanie needed to learn a lesson once and for all.

Chapter 6

FRANKiE

The spell was BACK ON! Tomorrow was opening night, and Heidi had to find the rest of the ingredients. She still needed:

◯	
	1 eye of a gingerbread man
	1 black plastic spider
	1 piece of straw

1 teaspoon of salt

3 cornflakes

2 sour gummy worms

1 puppy tooth

1 tablespoon of catnip

3 splashes of water

Heidi studied the list. *Candy will be easy,* she thought. She ran to the kitchen pantry and found the plastic Halloween pumpkins. She dumped the leftover candy on the floor and sifted through mini candy bars and loose candy corn. Then, like a glittering gem in a treasure chest, Heidi uncovered a black plastic spider.

"Yes!" said Heidi as she held up her find.

"Not so fast!" said Henry, who was standing in the doorway. "That's MINE."

"Finders keepers," said Heidi.

"Give it," said Henry. "Or I'll tell."

"Wait," said Heidi. "I'll trade my mini lightsaber I got at the Burger Pit."

"Done!" said Henry.

"It's on my nightstand," said Heidi.

Henry bolted upstairs.

Phew, thought Heidi. But she still needed sour gummy worms. Heidi's mother loved sour gummies— gummy worms, gummy bears, you

name it. Heidi tiptoed across the
kitchen and pulled open her mother's
secret candy drawer. She saw butter-
scotch candies and mints. *They have*

to be in here somewhere, she thought.
She reached farther into the drawer.
Her hand hit something. *Aha!* Heidi
pulled out a small crumpled bag from

the back of the drawer. She peeked inside. She saw red licorice and sour gummy worms.

"Score!" said Heidi.

She quickly stuffed two sour gummy worms into her pouch and one into her mouth.

"Heidi!" called Mom. "Time to go!"

Heidi shoved the bag back in the drawer.

"Okay!" said Heidi, trying to act normal.

Heidi had a playdate with Bruce.

He had asked her over to see his laboratory.

Mom drove Heidi to Bruce's house. He answered the door in his white lab coat and safety glasses. His puppy, Frankie, wagged his tail and barked at Heidi.

Heidi let Frankie sniff her hand.

"Has he lost any teeth yet?" asked Heidi.

"Not that I know of," said Bruce.

Heidi followed Bruce down to the basement. She looked around at all his experiments. Bruce had built a robot, and a tornado made out of

chicken wire and cotton balls. Some things were labeled TOP SECRET.

"Would you like to see how the Bicker Sticker works?" asked Bruce.

"Sure!" said Heidi.

Bruce tapped some keys on his computer. Heidi watched the screen. She saw something moving.

"That's Frankie," said Bruce.

Heidi couldn't see Frankie, but she could see what he was doing.

"Is he supposed to be eating hamburger buns?" asked Heidi.

Bruce looked closely at the screen.

"Oh no!" he said. "Come on!"

Heidi and Bruce raced up the stairs to the kitchen. There they

found Frankie happily munching on
hamburger rolls and wagging his tail.

Bruce tugged on the bag of rolls.
Frankie growled playfully.

"Give him a chew toy!" said Bruce.

Heidi spotted a basket of chew toys and grabbed a plastic pork chop.

"Here, Frankie!" said Heidi, waving the pork chop back and forth.

Frankie had no interest in the fake pork chop. He barked and whined at the hamburger rolls, which were now on the counter.

Heidi was about to toss the pork chop back into the basket when she noticed something stuck in the side. It was a tooth!

"I found a puppy tooth in the chew toy!" said Heidi.

"Let me see!" said Bruce.

Heidi picked the tooth out of the

pork chop and handed it to Bruce.

"That's so cool," said Bruce.

He pulled a magnifying glass out of his lab coat to get a better look.

"May I still trade you for a shark tooth?" asked Heidi. She tried not to sound too eager.

"Sure," said Bruce. "I'd much rather have a shark tooth any day."

He handed the tooth to Heidi, and she popped it into her pouch. Now she had nearly all the ingredients for her spell. Just three more to go, and a sand pail.

"I promise to bring a shark tooth to school tomorrow," said Heidi.

"Cool," said Bruce.

Then they thumped back down the stairs to the basement to check out some more science experiments.

Chapter 7

SHOWTiME!

Butterflies!

Jitterbugs!

Showtime!

Well, almost. Heidi had four hours
before opening night. She still had to
find a couple more spell ingredients.
The splashes of water would be easy.
So would the sand pail. The piece of

straw and the eye of a gingerbread man would be trickier.

After school Heidi's mother took Henry and Heidi to Lulu's Bakery. Mom

had ordered cupcakes for the cast party. Heidi prayed she would find the eye of a gingerbread man at the bakery. This would be her only chance.

Heidi stayed up front while Henry and Mom followed Lulu to the back of the store. When they were far enough away, Heidi turned to the lady behind the counter.

"Do you have any eyes for gingerbread people?" she whispered.

The lady thought for a moment. "They're out of season," she said, "but I'll check."

She opened and closed several little drawers. Then she pulled out a small strip of paper. The paper was dotted with tiny sets of candy eyes.

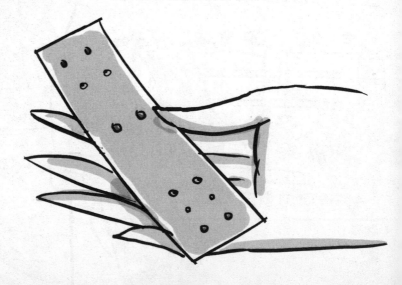

"How many do you need?" asked the lady.

"Just one," said Heidi.

"One eye?" asked the lady.

One eye *did* sound kind of strange.

"I mean, one pair," said Heidi.

"Here," said the lady. "Take what's left on the sheet."

"How much?" asked Heidi.

"No charge," said the lady, and she handed the strip of candy eyes to Heidi.

"Thank you!" said Heidi.

She gently folded the paper and put it in her pouch.

Lulu carried the cupcakes to the counter. Each cupcake had a *Wizard of Oz* topper.

"I want Toto!" said Henry.

"I want the ruby slippers!" said Heidi.

Heidi's mom paid for the cupcakes, and then they went home to pick up Dad.

"I forgot something in the house," said Heidi.

"Make it fast," said Mom. "You don't want to be late on opening night!"

Inside, Heidi carefully placed her pouch, her medallion, measuring spoons, a bottle of water, a spoon, and a pair of scissors in a shopping bag. Then she raced to the garage and unstacked the sand pails. She tossed a red one in the shopping bag. Then she zoomed to the cleaning closet and

plucked a bristle from the broom.

Oh no, thought Heidi. *These dumb bristles are made of plastic, not straw. How can a house with two witches have a fake broom?*

Heidi slammed the closet door behind her. She had everything she needed except for one crummy piece of straw. Now her spell was ruined. She grabbed her shopping bag anyway and ran to the car.

At school Heidi ignored everyone backstage. She put on her makeup and tree costume. Then she peeked around the curtain to see if Aunt Trudy had arrived. As she looked out at the audience someone pushed her from behind. Heidi stumbled onstage as Melanie and Stanley cracked up

behind the curtain. Heidi whirled around. She tried to find the split in the curtain, but all she found was more fabric. Then Lucy opened the curtain and yanked Heidi backstage.

"Are you okay?" asked Lucy.

Heidi wanted to scream. But then she looked at Stanley and got an idea.

"Help me out of my costume," said Heidi. "I have to use the bathroom."

Lucy lifted the tree trunk over Heidi's head.

"Hurry up!" said Lucy. "The play is about to start."

"I'll only be a sec," said Heidi.

Heidi grabbed her shopping bag. As she walked past Stanley she plucked a piece of straw from his scarecrow costume.

This will do the trick, she thought.

Then Heidi smiled wickedly.

Now she had everything she needed to cast her spell.

Chapter 8

THE SPELL IS ON!

Heidi hid in a bathroom stall and set the sand pail on the toilet seat. She peeled a candy eye from the strip of paper and dropped it in the pail. Then she added the spider, the straw, the gummy worms, the puppy tooth, and the three cornflakes.

Heidi measured
a teaspoon of salt
and added it to
the mix.

And then she
snipped a tiny
hole in the cat
toy and added
one tablespoon
of catnip.

102

She added three splashes of water and mixed the ingredients together with a spoon.

Then Heidi closed her eyes. She put her right hand over the pail and held the medallion in her left hand. Heidi chanted the words of the spell:

Oh special juice,
let your powers loose!
Help me quickly;
show me soon the signs.
Make Melanie Maplethorpe
forget her lines!

Now the joke will be on Melanie, thought Heidi.

Heidi gathered her things and headed backstage. The play had just started, and there was Melanie onstage, scratching her head. She couldn't remember her lines. The spell had worked!

Mrs. Noddywonks gave Melanie her opening line. "Oh, Toto," she said. "I wish I could go somewhere over the rainbow."

Melanie tried to repeat the words, but she forgot them again.

Kids backstage whispered and

laughed. Melanie's face turned red. She began to cry.

Mrs. Noddywonks ran onstage.

"Ladies and gentlemen," she said, "we're going to take a short break and be right back."

The curtain squeaked as it closed.

Mrs. Noddywonks put her arm around Melanie. "It's only the jitters," she said. "Take a deep breath."

"What's the matter with me?" Melanie wailed. "How did I become a terrible Dorothy?"

Just then something strange happened. Something so crazy, Heidi

had to pinch herself. She—Heidi
Heckelbeck—felt sorry for Melanie.

How can this be? she wondered.
Melanie is my worst enemy! But
Heidi couldn't bear to see Melanie so
upset. Heidi knew what that felt like,
and now she had made someone else
feel the same way. There was only
one thing to do.

A STAR IS BORN

Heidi ran back to the bathroom with her things. She entered a stall and set the red pail on the toilet seat. Heidi put her right hand over the pail and held her medallion in her left hand. Then she closed her eyes and reversed the spell.

Thank you.
Thank you.
Now all is well.
Undo my work
and reverse the spell.

As soon as Heidi walked out of the bathroom, she heard Melanie's voice.

"I remember my lines!" Melanie shouted.

"Oh good. . . . Thank heavens!" said

Mrs. Noddywonks. "Okay, children, take your places!"

After that, nobody tripped and no one forgot a single line.

At the end everyone came out onstage for their bows. Heidi could hear her dad cheering for her from

the audience. *The play wasn't so bad,*
thought Heidi. But she was glad it was
over!

"You were the best scary tree ever!" said Dad as he handed Heidi a cupcake with the ruby slippers on top.

"I want one too!" said Henry.

"Me too," said Mom.

"We'll be right back," said Dad as he, Mom, and Henry set off on a cupcake hunt.

Then Aunt Trudy gave Heidi a big hug.

"Isn't it a bit strange that Melanie forgot her lines?" asked Aunt Trudy. "And then suddenly—just like that— she remembered them! I can't explain it. Can you?"

Heidi looked at the floor. Aunt Trudy knew exactly what Heidi had done.

"Did you learn something?" asked Aunt Trudy.

"Yes," said Heidi. "It feels terrible to make someone unhappy."

"Good girl," said Aunt Trudy.

"But how come Melanie's mean to me?" asked Heidi.

"That's Melanie's problem," said Aunt Trudy. "Not yours. And hopefully someday Melanie will learn how to be kind too."

And that, along with her cupcake

with the ruby slippers on top, made
Heidi feel like a star.

Check out the next book starring

HEIDI HECKELBECK

HERE'S A SNEAK PEEK!

At school everybody was talking about the cookie contest.

Heidi walked over to her friend Lucy Lancaster. "What kind are *you* making?" Heidi asked Lucy.

"Sugar cookies," said Lucy. "With Fruity Polka Dots cereal on top."

An excerpt from *Heidi Heckelbeck and the Cookie Contest*

"Yum," said Heidi.

"What kind are *you* making?" asked Lucy.

"Chocolate chunk," said Heidi.

"Ew," said Melanie Maplethorpe. Melanie was Heidi's worst enemy. She had been listening in.

Heidi turned around. "What's your problem?" she asked.

"YOUR COOKIES!" said Melanie. "I mean, how blah can you get? Even Girl Scout cookies are more exciting than THAT."

Lucy put her hands on her hips and glared at Melanie. "What kind of cookies are *you* going to make?

An excerpt from *Heidi Heckelbeck and the Cookie Contest*

Disgusting chip? Or oatmeal poison?"

Melanie walked off with her nose in the air.

Heidi sighed. "It's true," she said. "My chocolate chunk cookies DO sound boring next to yours and Melanie's."

"Chocolate chunk cookies are NOT boring," said Lucy. "Stick with what you do best and you'll come out on top."

On top of what? thought Heidi. *The garbage heap? Maybe I need to come up with a fancier kind of cookie.* Heidi was sure of one thing: She had to outshine Melanie Maplethorpe.

An excerpt from *Heidi Heckelbeck and the Cookie Contest*